*All children have
a great ambition to read
to themselves...*
and a sense of achievement when they can
do so. The **read it yourself** series has been
devised to satisfy their ambition, and the
tales chosen are those with which children
are likely to be familiar.

Goldilocks
and the Three Bears

by Fran Hunia
illustrated by John Dyke

Ladybird Books Loughborough

Here are
the three bears.

4

This one is
the Daddy bear.

This one is
the Mommy bear.

And this one is
the baby bear.

They go
for a walk.

Here is Goldilocks.

No one is home,
says Goldilocks.

I can go in.

Goldilocks wants
some porridge.

Here is
Daddy bear's porridge.

It is too salty
for Goldilocks.

This is
Mommy bear's
porridge.

It is too sweet
for Goldilocks.

Here is
baby bear's porridge.

I like this porridge,
says Goldilocks.

Look.

Baby bear has
no porridge.

Goldilocks looks
for a chair.

This is
Daddy bear's chair.

It is too hard
for Goldilocks.

Here is
Mommy bear's chair.

It is too soft
for Goldilocks.

Here is
baby bear's chair.

I like this chair,
says Goldilocks.

Goldilocks sits down.

Look.

The chair has broken.

I want to go
to sleep,
says Goldilocks.

I can go up here.

Daddy bear's bed
is too hard.

Mommy bear's bed
is too soft
for Goldilocks.

Here is
baby bear's bed.

I like this bed,
says Goldilocks.

Goldilocks has a sleep.

The bears come home.

They go in.

Look, says baby bear.

The chair is broken.

I have no porridge,
he says.

The bears go up
to look for Goldilocks.

Up we go,
says Daddy bear.

Look,
says baby bear.
It is Goldilocks.

Daddy bear says,
Yes, it is Goldilocks.

Goldilocks jumps up.

You go home,
says baby bear.

Go home. Go home.